# CAPTAIN AWESOME

## MEETS SUPER DUDE!

By STAN KIRBY

Illustrated by GEORGE O'CONNOR

LITTLE SIMON

New York   London   Toronto   Sydney   New Delhi

LITTLE SIMON

An imprint of Simon & Schuster Children's Publishing Division • 1230 Avenue of the Americas, New York, New York 10020 • First Little Simon paperback edition June 2016 • Copyright © 2016 by Simon & Schuster, Inc. All rights reserved, including the right of reproduction in whole or in part in any form. LITTLE SIMON is a registered trademark of Simon & Schuster, Inc., and associated colophon is a trademark of Simon & Schuster, Inc. For information about special discounts for bulk purchases, please contact Simon & Schuster Special Sales at 1-866-506-1949 or business@simonandschuster.com. The Simon & Schuster Speakers Bureau can bring authors to your live event. For more information or to book an event contact the Simon & Schuster Speakers Bureau at 1-866-248-3049 or visit our website at www.simonspeakers.com. Designed by Jay Colvin. The text of this book was set in Little Simon Gazette.

Manufactured in the United States of America 0516 FFG 10 9 8 7 6 5 4 3 2 1

Cataloging-in-Publication Data for this title is available from the Library of Congress.

ISBN 978-1-4814-6696-7 (hc)

ISBN 978-1-4814-6695-0 (pbk)

ISBN 978-1-4814-6697-4 (eBook)

# Table of Contents

# CHAPTER 1

## Super Dude Saves The Day! Again!

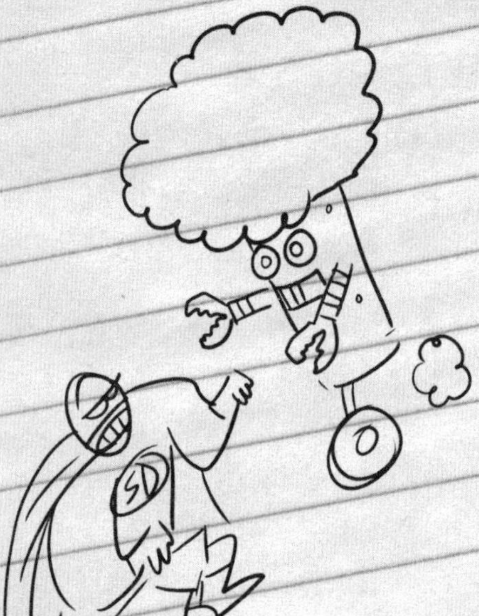

By Eugene

# BAM!
## *POW!*
## *LASER!*

Super Dude lasered the evil Ro-Broccoli right in the stalk. "Never again!" Super Dude vowed. "Never again shall you terrorize the peaceful citizens of Dudeville with your minerals and vitamins of terror!"

"You have not heard the last of

the bright green Ro—"But Ro-Broccoli was unable to finish his sentence.

## DOUBLE POW!

Super Dude popped the evil broccoli a powerful Dude-punch. Ro-Broccoli wobbled, and his eyes spun in different directions like twirling tops.

The robot vegetable who

planned to replace all the desserts on Earth with organic Broccoli-Bots fell into his bright green spaceship.

**SLAM!**

Super Dude kicked the door shut, lifted the spaceship off the ground, and hurled it into the air.

"Back to the intergalactic produce section with you!" he yelled in his most heroic voice ever.

The spaceship disappeared into the black hole over the Dudeville Clock Tower. Bright lights flashed across the sky as the black hole closed with one big space-sucking noise that sounded like the flush of a supertoilet.

The world
was saved. Again!
"Thank you,
Super Dude!" the
citizens cheered.
"You're welcome,
good citizens!" Super Dude

stood with his hands on his hips. His cape flapped in the breeze. "For the good people of Dudeville, there is nothing better than sending evil mutant robot broccoli right back to where it belongs. Now, who wants ice cream?!"

The Super Dude theme music started to play. The movie screen went black. The credits rolled.

Still wearing their 3-D glasses, the audience stood and cheered.

"*Super Dude versus Ro-Broccoli Three* was the best one yet!" yelled Eugene McGillicudy.

"Gotta stay for the end of the credits," his best friend, Charlie Thomas Jones, reminded him.

"There's always something cool at the end!" Sally Williams added.

They stared at the screen as the last credit rolled by.

And then Super Dude suddenly appeared on screen. He looked at the audience. "Hi, kids," he said.

"Don't forget that fighting evil is our number one mission. **KA-POW!**" Super Dude's foot came out of the screen in 3-D as he ka-pow kicked!

WHOA!

Eugene, Charlie, and Sally jumped back from their seats.

"That put all the Ds in 3-D!" Eugene said.

"I almost felt a breeze from the kick of the mighty Super Dude," Charlie exclaimed.

"Pow!" said Sally. "That was the greatest Super Dude movie yet!"

The kids dropped their popcorn buckets in the trash and left the theater. Eugene's mom was waiting to pick them up.

"That was the greatest Super Dude movie in the world!" yelled Charlie.

"That was the greatest Super Dude movie in the universe!" Eugene cried.

Wait a second.

What's that you say? You've never heard of Super Dude? But he's the superhero star of his own comic books, TV show, and movies, and is soon to be appearing in "Super Dude on Ice!" He once punched the sprinkles off the Cupcaker, who was trying to cover the world in chocolate frosting.

More important, Super Dude was the reason that Eugene, Charlie, and Sally joined together to become Sunnyview's own superheroes: the Sunnyview Superhero Squad.

As they left the theater, Eugene sighed. "Wouldn't it be awesome to meet Super Dude just once?"

"Sure would, Eugene," said Charlie.

"It's on my superhero To-Do list," Sally said. "That, and save the world!"

# CHAPTER 2

# Villains Galore!

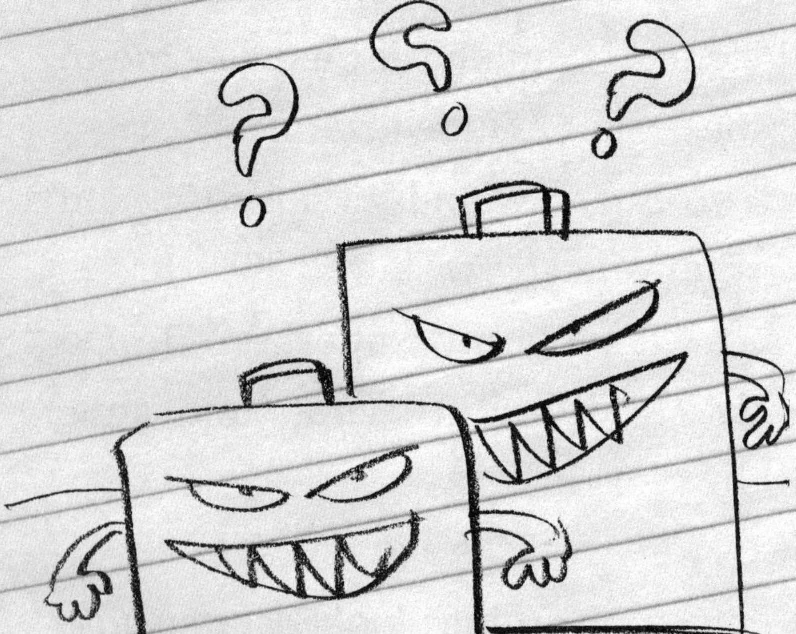

By Eugene

**S**omething evil was at the McGillicudys'. After dropping off Sally and Charlie, Eugene's mom pulled the car into their driveway.

As soon as she did, Eugene's Awesome-Sense tingled like a jingle bell caught in a spider's web.

Eugene scanned the yard and the sidewalk. He looked up at the big oak tree. Nothing was out of place. Nothing looked unusual.

He opened the car door.

**THUMP!**

The door bumped into something big. Something that
was waiting for him.

**LICK!**

And that
something was
furry and
it licked

Eugene right in the face. Only one supervillain ever *licked* victims in the face.

Mr. Drools!

NO!

Mr. Drools tried to push his drooling face into the car. Was he trying to come inside and smother Eugene with his toxic drool?

*I'm not even prepared!* Eugene thought.

That's right. Eugene was not prepared to fight evil. Thinking

that nothing bad could ever hap-
pen at a Super Dude movie, he had
left his Captain Awesome supersuit
in his bedroom, folded away in his
backpack. Eugene looked around
the car. He needed something to

distract Mr. Drools: an old French fry, a candy bar wrapper, or even a squeaky toy.

*How can I fight an evil Drool Dog from the Howling Paw Nebula without a distraction?*

*WAHHH!*

Eugene recognized that cry of doom.

Queen Stinkypants crawled from the house. Eugene's dad was right behind her. "Come back here!" he cried.

*Two* villains? Were Queen Stinkypants and Mr. Drools going to team up with some sort of

WAAA

double-drooling diaper attack?

WAAAAAAH!

Queen Stinkypants screamed her piercing baby scream as

Eugene's dad picked her up. Mr. Drools turned away from the car.

Perfect! Her evil scream was just enough to distract the dog. That was all the time Eugene needed. He ran from the car and dodged the evil Mr. Drools.

AAAA

"No drool for you this day, Mr. Drools!" Eugene shouted.

He made it to the front door faster than that time Super Dude beat the Speed Demon in Super Dude's Racing Spectacular No. 9.

"Thanks, Dad!" Eugene said. "You saved the day."

Sometimes all it takes to defeat

one villain is to distract it with another villain!

"How was the movie?" Eugene's dad asked. He held Queen Stinky-pants far from his nose in case she  unleashed a serious stinkbomb.

"It was only the greatest movie in the whole entire universe, including Mars, Jupiter, and Planet Ginormatron!" Eugene cried.

"Even better

than *Super Dude versus Mega Zombie Dude*?" Eugene's dad laughed.

"*Super* better!" Eugene replied.

"Well, you guys are home just in time to see Norm," Eugene's dad said.

Norm?

Eugene skidded to a stop. The name didn't ring any bells in his brain. *Who's Norm?*

"Eugene! Greetings!" Norm walked across the

lawn to the front door.

**GASP!**

Eugene remembered every-thing now.

"GASP!" He actually gasped. It was the gasp of horrible recognition. That wasn't just Norm, it was another archenemy of Captain Awesome: the evil Whistleblower!

*And he's here! At my house!* Eugene thought.

"Ready for soccer season? I just stopped by to see if you wanted to sign up for the team," The Whistleblower said.

A trick question! Eugene had to think fast. "Are *you* ready for soccer season?" he asked.

The Whistleblower frowned. "I asked you first," he said.

"I know you are, but what am I?!" Eugene replied.

"Okay, Eugene, maybe you should head inside," Eugene's dad said.

"You bet," said Eugene. He ran upstairs to his room. He reached under his bed.

## BACKPACK!
## UNZIP!

## CAPE!
## SUPERHERO!

Captain Awesome was downstairs in an action-packed minute. He leaped off the third stair and landed at the bottom. But he slipped on the rug and it carried him

across the floor with a *WHOOSH!*
Captain Awesome slid out the front
door and landed on the porch.

"You okay, Euge—I mean, Captain Awesome?" Eugene's dad asked.

"Oh, fine, sir," Captain Awesome replied. "I was just—where did The Whistle—I mean Norm, where did Norm go?"

"He had a soccer emergency," Eugene's dad said. He headed back inside with Queen Stinkypants.

Captain Awesome looked both ways down the street. "I'll get you next time, Whistleblower," he vowed.

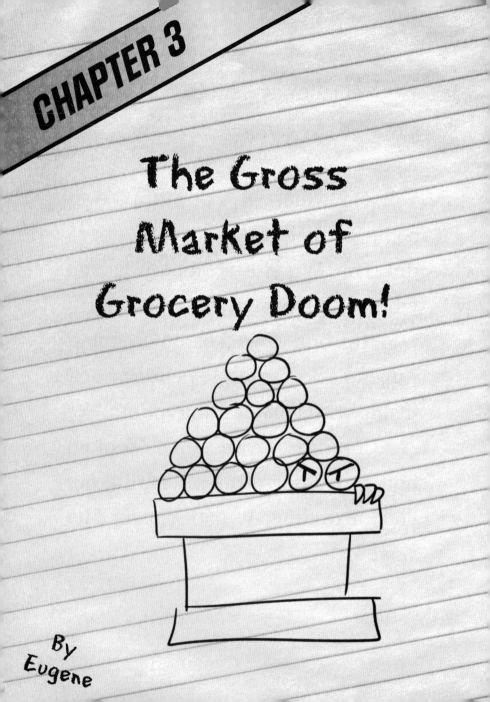

After breakfast the next morning, Eugene's mom said the most evil sentence ever: "We have to go to the grocery store."

NO!

The Gross Market of Grocery Doom was filled with gimonstrous aisles of organic asparagus, the deadly juice of the prune, and "healthy" cereals that tasted like wet cardboard!

"Do I have to?" Eugene asked his mom.

"Well, you *could* stay here on your own," Eugene's mom replied. "All alone. In the house. By yourself . . ."

*Well, now we're getting somewhere,* Eugene thought.

Until he thought about it some more. He realized there were three very big things wrong with his mom's stay-at-home plan:

1. Mr. Drools could attack again.

2. The garbage can filled with diapers of Queen Stinkypants could come to life.

3. The Whistleblower could return to flag Eugene with his Red Card of Destruction.

No, the Gross Market of Grocery Doom was the safest choice.

Or was it? Within two minutes, Eugene realized he should've stayed home. The market was the most boring place in Sunnyview. Even more boring than Professor Yawn, who kept making Super Dude sleepy in Super Dude No. 91.

The aisle with the recycled bamboo toilet paper? Boring.

The aisle with the gluten-free oatmeal-raisin cookies? Boring.

The aisle with the vegetables that *looked* like fruit? Tricky. Also boring!

But there was something very different just beyond the gorgonzola cheese.

*My Awesome sense sure is ring-ting-tingling!* Eugene thought. Eugene

looked up and saw the faces of two more of Captain Awesome's gallery of villains.

It was . . . the Double Dipper and the Raging Randonkey! And they had a cart full of organic food! Eugene was about to open his backpack and change into Captain Awesome, but then he remembered something really important about the Double Dipper.

After they first met, the Double Dipper turned out to not be so bad. In fact, he even liked Super Dude. And the Raging Randonkey was a

fan too. *People who like Super Dude can't be all bad,* Eugene remembered.

"Hey, Eugene!"the Double Dipper said. "You see the new Super Dude movie yet?"

"Just saw it,"Eugene responded with pride.

"Isn't it the best movie in the world?" said Randonkey.

"In the universe," corrected Double Dipper.

"Superlutely!" Eugene said. "Hey, what are you guys doing in the Gross Market of Grocery Doom?"

"Oh, we're cooking dinner for our girlfriends tonight," said Randonkey. "Roasted vegetables with okra, turnips, zucchini, and carrots."

Double Dipper added, "I'm making a pie for dessert!"

*Girlfriends? GROSS!* thought Eugene. *And cooking vegetables, too? Maybe these guys aren't so good after all.*

Eugene headed back toward his mom, who was trying to find a ripe cantaloupe, but he caught something out of the corner of his eye. An *orange* something peeking over a giant pyramid of oranges.

**COULD IT BE?**

Eugene watched as an orange-haired woman dressed in an orange jacket and matching orange pants squeezed oranges one after the other.

Eugene realized exactly who she was: the Orange Orangutango. She was going to squeeze all the

juice from the oranges and make kids drink the gross pulpy kind of orange juice! But Eugene was ready this time.

**BACKPACK!**
**UNZIP!**
**CAPE!**
**SUPERHERO!**

"I'm taking you down, Orange Orangutango!"

"My goodness!" The woman huffed at the sight of Captain Awesome. She backed away, bumping into the stack of oranges.

"Stop!" Captain Awesome yelled in his heroic "stop" voice. Captain Awesome was about to follow her, but one orange rolled off the pile. Then another. Then another. Then dozens came tumbling to the floor . . .

and kept coming. Captain Awesome tripped on an orange and fell. He tried to stand up. Oranges dropped into his lap and knocked him back to the ground.

"Euge—I mean Captain Awesome!" Eugene's mom gasped as

oranges rolled down the aisle. "Are you okay?"

"Did you see her?" Captain Awesome exclaimed. "She was here. The Orange Orangutango in all her orange-ish villain-ness!"

"I don't see anybody but you

and some oranges, honey," she said. "A lot of oranges."

She was right. Captain Awesome looked up and down the aisle. The Orange Orangutango was gone. He sighed. "I'll pick up the oranges."

Three villains were at his house yesterday, and now three more had shown up at the store.

*That's six villains in two days,* Eugene thought. Something *evil* was brewing in Sunnyview.

He was sure of it.

**CHAPTER 4**

# The Dinner Guest of Evil

By
Eugene

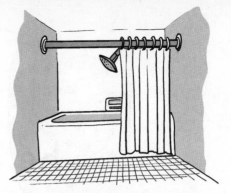

**E**ugene yanked open the closet door and dove in.

"I've got you now . . . coats?! Jackets?!" No villain was hiding inside the hallway closet.

Eugene ran into the bathroom and shoved aside the shower curtain. No villains in the bathroom either.

Eugene ran to the laundry room. Nothing in the washing

machine. But what about . . . the DRYER? Nope, nothing there either.

With his sweep of the house completed, Eugene sat down at the dinner table.

*GASP!*
*SHOCK!*
*BUNNY!*

There *was* a villain in his house and it was sitting right at the dinner table with his family! It wasn't the plate of asparagus in front of him—although that came in as a close second. No, it was the floppy

ears peeking over the edge of the table.

Those ears belonged to The Thumper, who was sitting next to Queen Stinkypants, giving Eugene the evil rabbit stare. The Thumper was using his dynamic Bunny Hop-nosis to make sure Eugene ate all his asparagus.

"Not tonight, Thumper!" Eugene cried. He jumped on top of

the table. "I'm sending you back to the Easter Pits of Bunnytopia once and for all!"

Eugene grabbed the bunny from Queen Stinkypants. He ran to the refrigerator and squeezed Thumper next to the egg carton. A superhero job well done.

Eugene turned back to his family. "Sorry," he said. "I don't

like bunnies watching me while I eat."

But then Queen Stinkypants unleashed her secret weapon: The Tears of Evil.

"*WAHHHHHHHHHHHHHHH. WAHHHHHHHHHHHHHHHHHH!*"

Eugene had to stop it before it destroyed the whole house . . . or

all of Sunnyview . . . or the world!
Once again, Eugene knew he had
to fight evil with evil. He went and
grabbed Thumper
from the fridge—
using tongs so
he didn't touch
the stuffed bunny.
Then he dropped
Thumper in Queen
Stinkypants's lap. It worked. She
stopped crying.

Eugene's mom smiled. "I have
a surprise for you, Eugene."

"Are we having chocolate

pudding with gummy worms and whipped cream for dessert?

Mrs. McGillicudy shook her head. "Nope. Better."

*Better? What could be better than chocolate pudding with gummy worms and whipped cream for dessert?* Eugene wondered.

"There's a Super Dude-tastic Super Party at the comic book store tomorrow," Mrs. McGillicudy said.

Eugene's mouth dropped open. A bite of asparagus fell out and landed on his plate. *How did I not know this?!*

"There may even be an appearance by Super Dude himself," Eugene's mom added.

"I—Charlie—but—Sally—what—I," Eugene lost the power to fit

words together in a sentence.

"I'll be taking you and Charlie and Sally," his mom explained, answering the question Eugene couldn't ask.

Then it hit Eugene like a bolt of lightning from the Lightning Bolt herself. Villains popping up all over Sunnyview! The Super Dude-tastic Super Party! The comic book store!

It was all making sense now.

Super Dude was going to be at the comic book store. All of Sunnyview's villains were uniting in some kind of Evil League of Get Together. There was a reason Eugene was running into them.

There was about to be a mega
hero versus villain superbattle at
the comic book store tomorrow.

Eugene had to warn Super Dude!

But how?

**HOW?!**

**G**ood morning, citizen! Rise and shine like a hero!"

Eugene's talking Super Dude alarm clock went off right at eight a.m. He bolted from the bed. There was no question about what he'd wear—he needed his Captain Awesome suit. Fortunately, he had slept in it.

Captain Awesome ran down the stairs two at a time. He wanted to eat fast and get to the comic book store early.

## DANGER! DANGER! DANGER!

There was something wrong in the house this morning. Captain Awesome sensed it right away.

There was no pancake smell. No delicious maple syrup fog blowing out of the kitchen. And no clatter of his dad

accidentally dropping the spatula on the floor.

It was very odd. More odd than that time in Super Dude No. 21 when Super Dude battled Oddball-boy, who could turn himself into a ball and bounce-bounce-bounce. That is, until he was swatted out of Dudeville by Super Dude's giant Baseball Bat of Good Swatting.

Maybe his family had been taken captive by alien cats from the planet Purrtron? Or the Celery

Stalker had risen from the Patch of Very Bad Vegetables and taken them?

"McGillicudys! Hey! Are you there? Are you anywhere?" Captain Awesome called out. "Activate Grid Search One," he added. "Operation Pancake has begun."

Captain Awesome ran from

room to room, opening every door and cabinet and cupboard and drawer. If his family was still here, he would find them.

But they were not to be found. There were no dishes in the sink. At the breakfast table he found nothing. In the toilet tank on the back of the toilet, he saw things no one should ever see.

HAHAHAHAHA!

"What was that?!" Captain Awesome stopped in the kitchen.

HAHAHAHAHA AGAIN!

It was coming from the back-yard. Captain Awesome crawled to the back door. There were people in the backyard, perhaps the ones who had kidnapped his family. "No backyard snatchers

will snatch my family or my pancakes!" he vowed.

"Beware, pure evil!" Eugene
yelled. He stood on the back porch
with his hands on his hips and

used his most heroic voice ever.
"Prepare to face the early morning
justice from the kick of Captain—
wait? What?"

Eugene's mom and dad were in

the backyard, sipping their morning coffee. Queen Stinkypants
wandered around on the grass,
probably looking for an alien ant
colony to rule.

"Good morning, Eug—I mean, Captain Awesome," Eugene's dad said.

Eugene's mom said, "We all got up early and decided to wait for you."

"I'm making my special bacon chocolate-chip pancakes," added his dad. "You'll need your strength if there's going to be trouble at the comic book store."

He was so right.

Captain Awesome's stomach rumbled. "Thank you, good citizen! Captain Awesome accepts your bacony offer."

Let's go, let's go, let's go!" Captain Awesome eagerly jumped into the backseat with Supersonic Sal and Nacho Cheese Man. "Commence Superhero Seatbelt Buckling!"

"Next stop: the comic book store!" Supersonic Sal called out.

Captain Awesome looked out the window. He was as excited as a dog discovering a superpowered treat-maker. And then he saw it. . . .

The old, spooky, haunted house the Sunnyview Superhero Squad had visited on Halloween night. **SHIVER!**

*But not even the Sunnyview*

*Spirit could stop me from getting to the comic book store today!* Captain Awesome thought.

The three heroes could barely stay seated when they passed Max Maxtone's Maxi Mini-Golf a few

miles later. Sure, it was the place Eugene, Sally, and Charlie had to suffer through Meredith's birthday party a few months ago, but it also meant that they were almost at . . .

### THE COMIC BOOK STORE!

Minutes later, the trio of heroes burst into the mall and immediately found themselves deep in a crowd of kids and parents who had come for the Super Dude party.

There were
kids dressed
as superheroes,
kids dressed as
sci-fi characters, kids
dressed as wizards
and witches, and kids

dressed as video game characters. The only thing there *wasn't*, was kids dressed as kids.

"Okay, heroes. I'll give you thirty minutes to complete your, uh, *mission*, then I've got a mission to get diapers for Molly." Eugene's mom took her place with the other parents who were sitting on the benches next to the comic book store.

"Keep those super eyes sharp," Captain Awesome whispered. "The supervillains could unleash their evil plan of no goodness at any moment!"

"I just hope they unleash it *after* we get Super Dude's autograph," Nacho Cheese Man replied.

"Captain Awesome!" a voice called out from the crowd.

Captain Awesome spotted a familiar superhero mask. "Amazing Man! I haven't seen you since Camp Ka-Pow!"

"I see you're still looking as *awesome* as ever," Amazing Man replied.

"And you're looking as *amazing* as ever," Captain Awesome replied.

Captain Awesome leaned closer to Amazing

Man and whispered, "Listen, my super Awesome-Sense warned me that a band of villains may be on their way to the comic store to get Super Dude."

"I hope they arrive *after* I get Super Dude's autograph," Amazing Man replied. "I'll be on the lookout. Cloudy Heights! Cloudy Heights! No evil shall escape my sight!"

No sooner had

Amazing Man disappeared into the crowd, then Captain Awesome's super Awesome-Sense started to tingle. "I sense danger!" he told his friends.

"Well, well, well. If it isn't Puke-Gene, Stinky Cheese Man, and Super-Lame-O Sal." Meredith Mooney pushed her way through the crowd.

"Meredith! That's not very nice!" Meredith's older sister, Melissa,

said. "Remember, I said I'd take you to see Kitty Rainbow and the Unicorn Band if you behaved while we were at the Super Dude-tastic Super Party."

"Fiiiiiiine," Meredith groaned, then secretly stuck her tongue out at Captain Awesome.

Music began to pump through the speakers and spotlights hit a small stage set up outside the comic book store.

### IT WAS TIME!

"IT'S DUPER SUUUUUUUDE! I MEAN SUPER SUUUUUUUUDE! I MEAN POOPER MOOOOOOD! I . . . I . . . MEAN . . . SUPER

DUUUUUUUUUUUUUUDE!"
Nacho Cheese Man was so excited,
he could barely stop his head from
exploding from the 110 percent,
hyper-overdrive Super Dude awesomeness!

Super Dude had arrived!

# CHAPTER 7

# The Ewwwww of Evil!

By Eugene

Super Dude stepped onto the stage and waved a mighty hand to the fans squished together like marshmallows in a hamster's cheek. Cries of "Super Dude! Super Dude!" filled the air.

But Captain Awesome was silent. He rubbed his eyes. He had seen plenty of cardboard Super Dudes before. And tons of stuffed Super Dudes. He had seen Super

Dude in video games and on tooth-brushes, posters, cereal boxes, pillows, blankets, lunch boxes, and phone cases. He had seen Super Dude's smiling face on pretty much everything you could buy online, on TV, or in a store. He'd even seen

Super Dude Frozen Peas once—but even *that* couldn't make him eat those terrible green pearls of grossness.

Captain Awesome had also seen plenty of *people* dressed as Super Dude. But each time, something was always off: Super Dude's cape wasn't capey enough, or his belt wasn't super enough, or his mask wasn't dude enough.

There was always something . . . *something* that made it easy for Captain Awesome to spot an imposter. But this time . . . this time Super Dude looked *exactly* like Super Dude.

EMERGENCY MEETING!

Captain Awesome quickly huddled with Nacho Cheese Man and Supersonic Sal.

"We've gotta figure out if this is the real Super Dude so we can warn him that the bad guys want to get him!" Captain Awesome explained.

"Let's ask him questions that only the real Super Dude would know the answers to," Supersonic Sal suggested.

"We can see if he has Super Dude's Super Villain Super Sense," Nacho Cheese Man added.

"And the *final* test can be to see if he can . . . SAVE THE UNIVERSE!" Captain Awesome added with dramatic flair.

"How can he do that if the universe isn't in danger?" Nacho

Cheese Man asked.

"If he's really Super Dude, he'll figure something out," Captain Awesome replied.

Before Captain Awesome could say another word, Nacho Cheese Man grabbed his arm. "Look!" he stammered and pointed across the mall.

It was The Shusher, the evil rule-maker of the school spelling bee. She was with the Freeze Tagger, the supervillain who patrolled the Sunnyview Museum with his freeze ray!

"They must be here to kidnap Super Dude!" Captain Awesome gasped.

The heroes were about to

charge into action, but then they saw something even more horrible than the spinach mines of Veggietopia. The Shusher and the Freeze Tagger were *holding hands*!

"Ewwwwwwwwwwwww!" Captain Awesome and Nacho Cheese Man said in unison. Captain Awesome noticed Supersonic Sal was smiling and not "ewing," so he elbowed her.

"What? Oh, yeah, um, EW!"
Supersonic Sal joined in.

"I don't think they're here to do
anything except make me puke,"
Nacho Cheese Man said.

# CHAPTER 8

# The Fast and the Curious

By
Eugene

All right! Who's next in line for a Super Dude Autograph?!" Super Dude looked to Captain Awesome. "What's your superpower—"

"How did you defeat the Kitty Litterer?!" Captain Awesome asked.

"Well, I—"

Supersonic Sal immediately cut off Super Dude and asked, "Who made you make all the lava beds in

the land Volcania?!"

"What's your favorite pasta sauce!?"Nacho Cheese Man snapped.

The questions came fast and furious! Super Dude had nowhere to turn . . . nowhere to run!

"Where did El-Sucko hide his power-sucking ray?!"

"What disguise did you use to save the Cauliflower Kid from the Cabbage Patchitorium of Baron Broccoli?"

"Who's the world's angriest sea mammal?!"

"Who did you defeat with the

buttery goodness of goodness?"

"What kind of action awesomeness does the Super Dude action figure have?"

"How did you defeat the Exclamation Pointer and free Grammartopia?" Captain Awesome asked. Then he leaned closer to a clearly overwhelmed Super Dude. *"Well?!"*

The crowd fell silent. Super Dude gritted his teeth. He squinted his eyes, adjusted his cape, and laughed nervously. Then he cleared his throat.

"A giant ball of string. Dr. Chore. The Human Tomato's Atsa Lotsa Pasta Sauce. Stinky blue cheese. A turnip. The Water Weasel. Colonel Kernel.

Dude-Jitsu. And I kicked the Exclamation Pointer right in the dangling participle!"

Captain Awesome, Nacho Cheese Man, and Supersonic Sal stood in stunned silence as the crowd erupted in cheers.

"That's what makes him so super," Nacho Cheese Man said in awe.

"He still has two more tests to go," Captain Awesome whispered, overcoming his shock. "First, does he have Super Dude's Super Villain Super Sense?" Captain Awesome motioned to Meredith, who stood in line directly behind them.

Meredith pushed

her way past Captain Awesome. "Outta my way, Puke-Gene! My sister wants to meet Super *Dud* so we can get outta here."

"That's Super *Dude*, little miss," Super Dude politely corrected.

"Not from where I'm standing," Meredith said.

"Why, aren't *you* the sweetest little pink princess," Super Dude said with a smile. "You know, pink is my favorite color."

"Well, get a *new* favorite, 'cause pink is *mine*," Meredith sneered.

"'Sweet?!' 'Pink?!' 'Princess?!'" Captain Awesome whispered to Nacho Cheese Man and Supersonic Sal with gross-gustedness, which anyone who had to deal with Meredith knew was a combination of grossness and disgust. "There is no way Super Dude would ever say those things about someone as villainous as Meredith!"

Super Dude signed an autograph for a very thankful—and
even more embarrassed—Melissa.
As Meredith and Melissa walked
away, he leaned over to Captain

Awesome and whispered, "I could smell the evil on that kid like stink on an evil baby!"

"Then why were you so nice to her?" Captain Awesome asked.

"Because there's no greater superpower than kindness," Super Dude said.

"That's what makes him so super...," Nacho Cheese Man said in awe.

"You already *said* that," Captain Awesome rolled his eyes.

"Well, it's still true," Nacho Cheese Man replied.

"That's two tests passed and one to go," Supersonic Sal reminded them.

"The *last* test should be the easiest one of all for Super Dude," Captain Awesome said. "He just needs to save the universe. Although, I suppose saving the world would be okay."

"Well, I hope the world needs saving soon," Nacho Cheese Man said. "Your mom is taking us to buy diapers in five minutes!"

**N**acho Cheese Man was right. Eugene's mom motioned to her watch. Time was running out.

"Where's a giant meteor or an alien invasion when you need one?" Captain Awesome asked.

And then it happened!

***CRACKLE!***
***SQUEAL!***
***SNAP!***

"Hey, guys, what was that?"

Supersonic Sal asked.

"I don't know," Captain Awesome replied. "But it kinda sounded like it came from the sky. . . ."

"Like an ALIEN INVASION!" Nacho Cheese Man gasped.

The trio of heroes looked up, hoping to see a fleet of aliens blast through the mall's ceiling.

But instead of an invasion they heard . . . THE VOICE!

"Happy smiles, Sunnyview shoppers! I hope you're all having a rainbow-tastic shopping day!" a syrupy voice said over the mall's loudspeakers.

Captain Awesome covered his ears. "Have you ever heard a more evil voice?!"

Nacho Cheese Man fell to his knees. "All the sweetness is giving me a brain cavity!"

"Can't get the rainbow-tastic-ness out of my head!" Supersonic Sal grabbed her head. The announcement continued: "Meow! Meow! Meow! I'm

Kitty Rainbow and I'm here with my Unicorn Band to put on a concert!"

Then came a sound even more brain-melting than Kitty Rainbow's voice.

"EEEEEEEEEEEE!" Meredith shrieked. "I wanna see Kitty Rainbooooooow! I wanna! I wanna! I wanna!"

"And *I* wanna get outta here!"
Nacho Cheese Man said as other
kids squealed along with Meredith.

And then *more* happened!

### SPEAKERS!
### LIGHTS!
### DISCO BALL!

Kitty Rainbow and the Unicorn
Band raced onto the stage like a
glittery pink nightmare!
Kitty Rainbow's face was
painted like a pink cat.
Her four Unicorn Band
members wore unicorn horns on
their heads and pranced around

the stage as if they'd just escaped from a My Tiny Pony poster.

"I'm sliding on a rainbow! I'm meowing in the sun! Prancing pink unicorns having lots of fun! Dance with me! Prance with me! Everybody get pinky, pink, pink with me!" Kitty Rainbow sang.

"This is eas-ily the most evil thing I've ever seen or heard," said Supersonic Sal, horrified.

"But you gotta admit, it's kind of a catchy song," Nacho Cheese Man said as he tapped his foot to the beat.

"Fight it, Nacho Cheese Man!" Captain Awesome warned. "Kitty Barfbow is trying to turn us all into . . . Zom-pinkies!"

"I don't know what that is, but I hate it already!" Nacho Cheese Man covered his ears to block out the music.

"If we can't stop Kitty Barfbow and the Unicorn Barfers," Captain Awesome began, "It'll be the END OF THE WORLD!"

# CHAPTER 10

# The End of the World!

By
Eugene

**N**acho Cheese Man covered his ears even tighter. "I can . . . feel my brain . . . turning pink!"

"Must fight the urge . . . to play with ponies!" Supersonic Sal stammered.

"This must be . . . the bad guys big plan . . . to kidnap Super Dude!" Captain Awesome managed to say.

Even Mr. Dooms, the substitute teacher that the kids thought

was a supervillain
(he wasn't), was at the
mall. He was happily
bouncing to the beat,
unaware that he was
being turned into
a Zom-pinky by
Kitty Rainbow's
awful song.

"Isn't this
the best
thing you've ever heard?" Meredith
shrieked with delight and sang,
"Get pinky, pink, pink with me!"

"AAAAAAAAHHH!" the three

heroes screamed in unison and ran away.

"I don't want to get pinky, pink, pink with anyone!" Nacho Cheese Man said worriedly as they hid under a table.

"We need to do what we always do when we need to do something!" Captain Awesome said. "And that's

'Do what Super Dude would do!'"

"He'd use his Super Minty Breath and blow Kitty Barfbow away with minty freshness!" Supersonic Sal said.

"We can't! I was so excited I forgot to brush my teeth this morning," Captain

Awesome replied. "But remember how Super Dude defeated Justin Eel-er and Eely Cyrus when they tried to sing their electric eel duet of doom at the Super Dude Waterslide?"

"He teamed up with Codzilla and had his pet Slobster drool on them?" Nacho Cheese Man asked.

"Nope! I unplugged those slimy do-badders and sent them both to the aquarium in a clambulance!" a voice behind the three heroes said.

Captain Awesome turned to see Super Dude standing behind them.

"You guys ready to save the universe?" Super Dude asked. "Or at least the world?"

## TEST NUMBER THREE!

"Okay, if he does save the world, then he's really Super Dude," Captain Awesome reminded Supersonic Sal and Nacho Cheese Man in a whisper.

Without another word, Super Dude pulled the huge yellow power cord from the wall.

Suddenly . . . the lights went out! The disco ball stopped spinning! The mind-melting Zom-pinky music faded. Hundreds of kids groaned in dismay, and no one louder than Meredith.

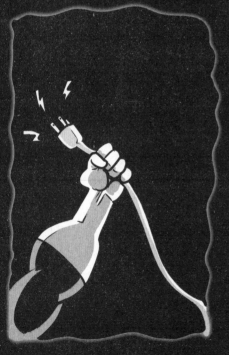

Captain Awesome, Nacho Cheese Man, and Supersonic Sal gasped.

"You just saved the universe!" Nacho Cheese Man exclaimed.

"Or at least the world!" Supersonic Sal cried.

"You really *are* Super Dude!" Captain Awesome said in shock.

"In the flesh. Or should I say, in the Spandex," Super Dude

admitted. "I've been pretending to pretend to be Super Dude all day. It's nice to just be me, finally."

*"Pretending to pretend to be . . ."* Nacho Cheese Man's head began to spin.

"You superheroes have been doing some MI-TEE superheroing here in Sunnyview," Super Dude said.

"How . . . how did you know?" Captain Awesome stammered.

"Even a cloudy day can't stop me from seeing the rays of goodness!" Super Dude explained. "And

no heroes in Sunnyview shine brighter—or gooder—than you three."

Super Dude lifted the power cord plug. "Now, how about we plug this back in? I think Kitty Rainbow learned her lesson and there'll be no more turning *anyone* into Zompinkies."

Captain Awesome gave a nod. Super Dude plugged the cord back into the wall. The lights came on. The disco ball spun. Kitty Rainbow's music filled the air. Hundreds of kids started screaming again, and no one louder than Meredith.

"I know you've had some tough battles. But as I said in Super Dude Number 26 when I battled Frank Einstein and his furry EMC Bears: 'Sometimes there's evil to be battled, and sometimes there's evil that's not *really* evil after all.'"

Super Dude gave a nod. Captain Awesome, Nacho Cheese Man,

and Supersonic Sal turned to see Meredith jumping up and down to Kitty Rainbow's music and squealing like a pink pig in a pink mud puddle.

"Everyone's entitled to their own opinion," Nacho Cheese Man whispered to his two heroic friends.

Later that night, Eugene put his autographed copy of the newest Super Dude comic book in his super-secret underwear drawer so Molly couldn't drool on it. He plopped on his bed, still smiling from the events of the day.

"I can't believe it, Turbo. I finally met the REAL Super Dude," Eugene said.

*Squeak, squeak, squeak,* Turbo squeaked his hamster squeak.

"No. It was better than that! It was, like, a billion, jillion, kazillion times better than that. It was . . . it was . . ." Eugene paused as he tried to find the perfect word to express what it was like to meet his idol. And then he realized there was only one possible way to describe it:

"It was . . . MI-TEE!"

Don't miss the next
Captain Awesome adventui

# CAPTAIN AWESOME
## HAS THE BEST SNOW DAY EVER?

One morning everyone's favorite superhero awakens to something suspicious. His mom's not calling him to come downstairs for breakfast and his school clothes aren't laid out for him. He peeks out the window and gasps. He can barely see anything through the piles and piles of . . . snow! This can only mean one thing. SNOW DAY! And it's going to be the best snow day ever! Or is it?